For Tara Walker,
in gratitude and with affection
— C.F.

For all the bears who want to sing
— D.S.

Tundra Books, an imprint of Penguin Random House Canada Young Readers,
a division of Penguin Random House of Canada Limited

LIBRARY AND ARCHIVES CANADA CATALOGUING IN PUBLICATION

Title: Bear wants to sing / written by Cary Fagan ;
illustrated by Dena Seiferling.
Names: Fagan, Cary, author. | Seiferling, Dena, illustrator.
Identifiers: Canadiana (print) 20200297163 | Canadiana (ebook) 20200297171
ISBN 9780735268036 (hardcover) | ISBN 9780735268043 (EPUB)
Classification: LCC PS8561.A375 B43 2021 | DDC jC813/.54—dc23

Published simultaneously in the United States of America by Tundra Books
of Northern New York, an imprint of Penguin Random House Canada Young
Readers, a division of Penguin Random House of Canada Limited

LIBRARY OF CONGRESS CONTROL NUMBER: 2020942687

Edited by Tara Walker with assistance from Margot Blankier
Designed by John Martz
The artwork in this book was rendered in graphite and colored digitally.
The text was set in Goudy Old Style.

Printed in China

www.penguinrandomhouse.ca

1 2 3 4 5   25 24 23 22 21

Penguin
Random House
tundra | TUNDRA BOOKS

BEAR
WANTS TO
SING

WRITTEN BY Cary Fagan & ILLUSTRATED BY Dena Seiferling

tundra

A bear was taking a walk.

He saw something in the grass.

He sniffed it.

He licked it.

He picked it up and plucked it.

It made a nice sound.

Plink!

The bear turned around, eager to show
somebody.

A mouse was sitting on a stump,
washing his tail.

"Look!" said the bear. "I'm a musician.
I want to sing you my song."

The mouse crossed his legs and put his
paws in his lap.

"I'm all ears," he said.

Just then a crow landed beside them.
"What's going on here?"

"I'm a musician," said the bear.
"And I'm going to sing my song."

The crow stepped on something.
It made a delicious rattle.

"A tambourine!" said the crow.
"Let *me* sing first."

And before the bear could protest,
the crow began to strike the instrument
with her foot.

Never mind your jay, your robin or your owl,

Your chickadee or grouse or any kind of fowl.

Birds of a feather, up high or down low —

None are as fine as the clever crow!

"That is a good song,"
the bear said grumpily.

"*Pretty* good," said the mouse.
"Now let's hear yours, Bear."

A snake came slithering through
the grass. "What are you doing?"

"I am a musician," said the bear.
"I have a song and I'm going to sing it."

"Wait, what's this?" asked the snake.
She parted the grass to reveal a small
drum.

She thumped on the drum with her tail
and began to sing.

The ground's a lovely place, you know,

To slink and slither to and fro.

But even better is to creep

Under a rock for a nice, long sleep.

"Hmm," said the bear.
"That's a good song too."

"Go ahead, Bear," said the mouse.
"It was your turn before and it's your
turn now."

Blaaaaaaat!

They all turned to see a tortoise nearby.
He was standing on a rock and holding
a horn.

"Look what I found," he said.
"What a noise it makes!
Now I can play *and* sing."

"Really, Tortoise," said the mouse,
"you ought to wait your turn."

But the tortoise had already begun.

There's a well-known saying — Blaaat! — and it goes like this:

There's simply no place — Blaaat! — like home.

But a tortoise — Blaaat, blaaat! — has his own cozy place

Wherever he happens to roam!

Blaaaaaaaaaaaaaaaaaat!

A fox emerged from the bushes.

"I've been listening to you all," she said.
"Most impressive indeed. I suggest that
we start a band. We could go to town and
play on stage. I will be your manager."

"A band!" cawed the crow.

"We'll be famous!" hissed the snake.

"Count me in!" wheezed the tortoise.

"I believe you're getting ahead of
yourself," said the mouse.
"Bear has not sung his song yet."

"I don't feel like it anymore,"
said the bear.

"Please do," said the tortoise.

"Yes," said the fox.
"The band needs another song."

"Well," said the bear, blushing a little,
"if you insist."

He twitched his nose,
strummed the instrument,
and opened his mouth.

I'm a bear, I'm a bear, I'm a bear, I'm a bear,

I'm a bear, I'm a bear, I'm a bear, I'm a bear,

I'm a bear, I'm a bear, I'm a bear . . .

I'm a BEAR!

The bear gave one last strum.

"What do you think?" he asked.

"Well," said the crow, "it certainly . . . why, it certainly gets to the point."

"And it's — well, let me think," said the tortoise. "It's easy to remember."

"Very easy," agreed the snake.

The bear sighed heavily.

"You didn't like it." He put down the instrument and lumbered off.

Through the grass went the bear,
over a hill, between some trees,
and down to the river.

The mouse followed.

The bear waded into the water.

"Where are you going?" asked the mouse.

"Far away," said the bear.

"For how long?"

"Forever. Well, almost forever."

The bear floated on his back.

The mouse crouched down, hopped into the air, and landed on the bear.

They floated along, the mouse sitting on the bear's belly.

"I like your song," said the mouse.

"You do?" asked the bear. "Why?"

"Because it is just like you."

The mouse lay down on the bear's belly.

As the bear breathed, the mouse went up
and down.

"*I'm a bear,*" sang the mouse quietly.

"*I'm a bear, I'm a bear, I'm a bear . . .*"

The bear smiled. "*I'm a mouse,*" he sang.

"*I'm a mouse, I'm a mouse, I'm a mouse . . .*"

The mouse chuckled.

The two of them sang together, looking
up at the clouds as they floated down
the river.